ROSE JOHNSON

Lost Goddess

Copyright © 2023 by Rose Johnson

All rights reserved. No part of this publication may be reproduced, stored or transmitted in any form or by any means, electronic, mechanical, photocopying, recording, scanning, or otherwise without written permission from the publisher. It is illegal to copy this book, post it to a website, or distribute it by any other means without permission.

This novel is entirely a work of fiction. The names, characters and incidents portrayed in it are the work of the author's imagination. Any resemblance to actual persons, living or dead, events or localities is entirely coincidental.

Rose Johnson asserts the moral right to be identified as the author of this work.

First edition

This book was professionally typeset on Reedsy. Find out more at reedsy.com

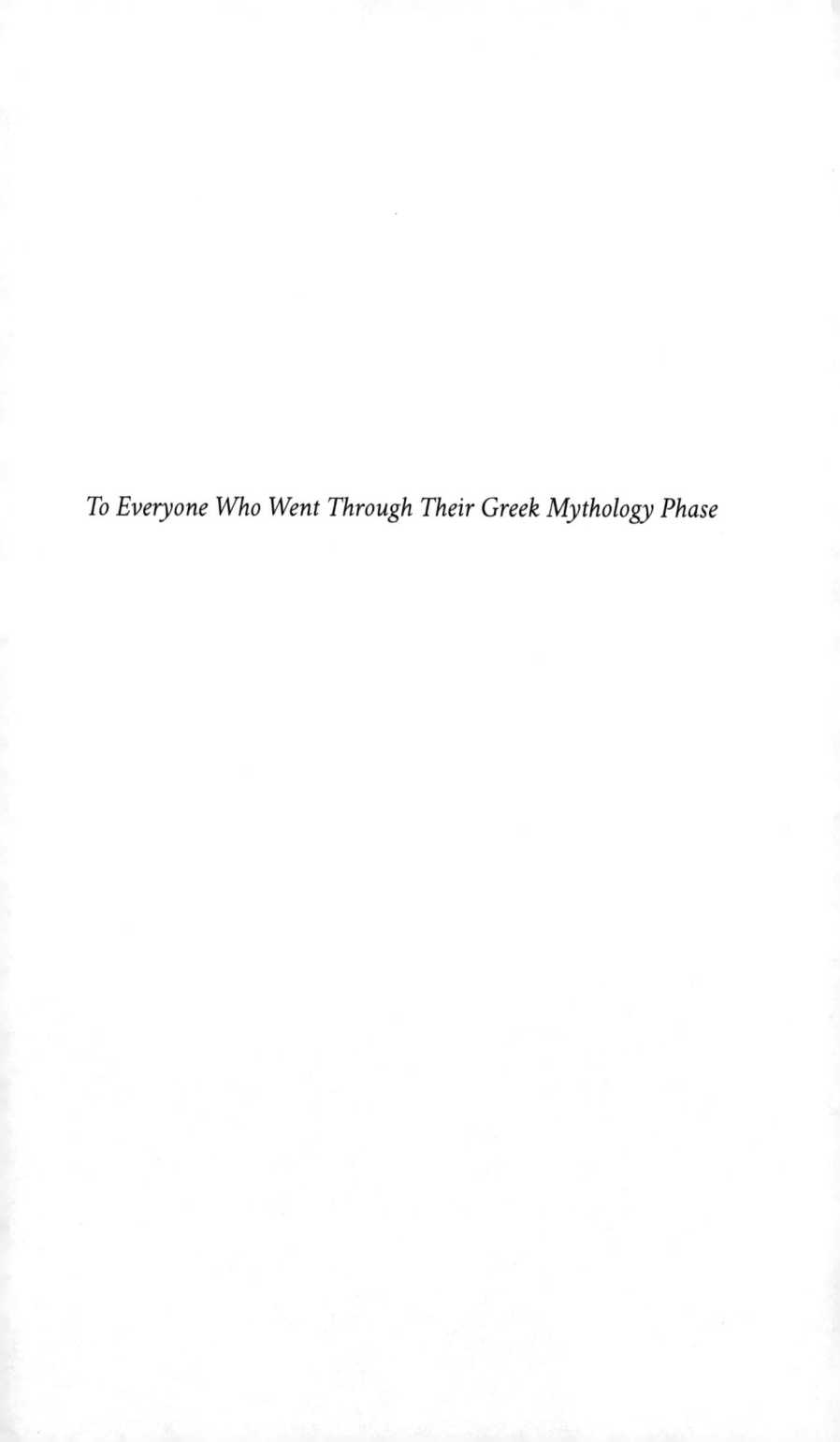

To Everyone Who Went Through Their Greek Mythology Phase

Contents

Foreword	ii
Chapter 1	1
Chapter 2	5
Chapter 3	8
Chapter 4	13
Chapter 5	16
Chapter 6	20
Chapter 7	23
Chapter 8	31
Chapter 9	35
Chapter 10	38
Chapter 11	43
Chapter 12	46

Foreword

Trigger Warnings Include: mild violence, poisoning, overall some toxicity, best friend's dad

Chapter 1

It was exactly three weeks before I graduated from university. I was on my way to freedom.

Besides that, there wasn't anything special about today. The trees shone with every color of green. I noticed the colors of things a lot, it comes with the territory of being Iris's daughter.

You see, many of the gods had declared themselves a few decades ago and settled down on Earth to live lives here. They married, had children, started companies. I was one of these children, a child of Iris.

It was early morning when Haidar found me standing on top of the university park's hill. I had been thinking for hours.

Recently, Anna Artemis had asked me to join her woman's society. She said that although I was a bit young to join the organization, she still would be pleased if I joined them.

She had given me a deadline: I had to join before I graduated. There was also, of course, the case of leaving Haidar and all my other friends. If I accepted Anna's invitation ,when would I see them again? "Hey, looking for anything in particular?" Haidar asked.

"Not really, just enjoying the park's peace," I answered.

"Peace. That's a funny concept."

"Funny how?" I asked her.

"Just seems there is always drama." Her eyes welled with tears.

"Not at this moment. Look, just us and the forest. Nothing else exists," I reassured her.

"I can see that. It is pretty. Prettier to you, I guess."

"Only because of biology, though."

"So... around noon, some of us are going on a hunt," she began. "I was wondering if you wanted to come with? Your archery skills could really help."

"That sounds great..." I forced a smile back at her. I fidgeted my hands. "Any... um, any news from Simon?" I asked.

Simon. Damn Simon. I loved him. I hated that I loved him. I didn't leave my room for a week when he left for the quest. He knew it was dangerous and he left anyway. At that time I hated him for it. Then about three months ago, we had lost contact with his crew. I could only assume the worst, but I wanted to believe that he would return. He promised that he *would*.

"Not yet." She patted me on the shoulder.

Simon was the biggest reason I hadn't joined the women's coalition yet. It was a hundred miles away and I couldn't bear the thought of losing Simon.

"Oh." My head hung low.

"Miss him?" she asked.

I nodded. "Funny, isn't it? I was constantly rejecting him, but the moment he is gone, I can't help but miss him."

Haidar leaned her head on my shoulder. "I think it's perfectly reasonable."

Chapter 1

"Thank you… and if you do hear from him…," I began.

"I'll tell you instantly." Haidar was the best friend slash sister I could ever ask for. As kids, we were put into the same foster home and we'd stuck together ever since.

"Do you know what day it is?" she asked, staring at the ground as she kicked some rocks.

I shook my head.

"It's the anniversary of the day Apollo lost Daphne. The woods are full of magic today." She nudged me with her arm.

Hunting always cleared my mind, and that's exactly what I needed. Haidar probably noticed that I was trying to find peace because she left after that, leaving me alone in my thoughts.

I glanced down at my watch and realized that what had felt like five minutes had truly been two hours. I only had fifteen minutes to prepare for the hunt. I ran as fast as my feet could carry me through the camp to my cabin.

I stopped to glance at my brothers' beds. Later in life I found my bio brothers. We all shared the same mom and they used to live in these very dorms. I love my brothers. They have been there for me since the day we met when I was sixteen. I have never been jealous over the fact that they communicate with our dear mother. They have never looked down on me for not having all the powers they do. They are my true family, my true protectors.

Somehow, all my brothers grew up alone. All our fathers left us, and so while other people have families outside of the alumni community they can go home to, making their half-siblings less like siblings and more like uni friends, my brothers and I are the only family any of us have.

This has made us very close, and I always know that at the end of May, I can go home to my older brothers, especially Lyle.

Four years ago, he legally became my guardian and I couldn't have been happier.

When I got inside the dorm, I ran quickly to my bunk and put on my hunting clothes. The dress stopped right above my knee and the bodice was leather that covered even my shoulders. The skirt had strips of leather to stop any of my loose arrows from ripping the cotton underneath. Most of the other hunters preferred camouflage or full body armor, but I was perfectly happy with my dress. It allowed me to move freely through the woods.

When I glanced down at my watch, I realized I was already late for the hunt. There was no time to gather my weapons or put my hair up. I just ran towards the woods praying that I could find the hunters before whatever we were hunting found me.

Chapter 2

Haidar was right, there was a strange air in the forest today. I had the feeling that both something sinister and something beautiful was hiding in here, and that something or someone was watching me, it sent shivers down my spine. It was like the magic swirled around me as I walked, full of inconsistencies, cold yet warm, loud yet oddly quiet..

I tried to ignore the feeling, but it kept pestering me. Eventually, I convinced myself that it must be a harmless squirrel or bird watching me and kept moving.

I loved the tranquility of the forest. This was where I truly felt at home. The trees above me were hundred-year-old monuments that represented how the world had changed. No tree was the same, and none stayed the same. Each year they grew wider and higher, reaching for the heavens.

It wasn't just the trees that made me feel at home. Everything from the whistling blades of grass to the thousand-colored flowers seemed to call out to me, to ask me to stay.

Lost Goddess

After thirty minutes or so I came to a cliff, overlooking a small but glistening lake below. It was clear that I was not going to find the hunters anytime soon. Something in me felt like I should stop there and take a swim. I didn't know why, and I didn't need to.

When I reached the bottom I unstrapped my sandals and took off my hunting dress. Still covered by a black tank top and green Nike shorts, I waded into the lake.

The coolness of the lake was refreshing after trudging through dense woods.

The more I walked the more I could feel eyes on me. I quickly decided to ignore the feeling and kept swimming.

After a while I decided to get out and set my feet in the water, allowing the rest of me to dry on a bed of sand.

Laurels surrounded the lake, and it reminded me of how Apollo lost Daphne. I was unsure if the story was meant to grow sympathy for Apollo or hatred for him for pursuing someone who rejected him, but I had always liked it.

I recalled a song that Haidar commonly sang when we were kids. The name was something like *Apollo's Fight*. Wait... not *Fight*... *Plight* was the word. *Apollo's Plight*.

Laying on my back, eyes closed, I started to sing the song in my head. Before I got to the second line I was singing aloud.

"Eros why do you hate me so
Your arrow struck me with a hard blow
My love hated me
Her fear brakes me

Why does my love flee from my touch
Her embrace is all that I want
From the moment I saw her hunting alone

Chapter 2

I knew I wanted her to come to my home"

At this point another voice joined mine. The voice was obviously masculine, but it was gentle, unlike any other voice I had ever heard. As the voice sang with me, I felt peaceful, but I was also in shock and afraid to open my eyes. I wanted to move away, but I felt glued to the ground.

"All I wish for is her embrace
To feel her lips upon my face
But alas this is my fate
To be alone for all my days

But that fate I will not accept
So I pursued her to the death
And when I finally felt her touch
She fled far from my love

I followed her to the edge
And a tree sprang from her legs
Forever my love lost to me

And forever her part of my victory"

I froze at the end of the verse.

Chapter 3

I shot up immediately and looked at the person next to me. "Simon?" I mouthed as I looked down at the man. Wait. I looked closer. Same build as Simon, similar blonde hair, but different eyes, a stronger cupid's bow. No— this person wasn't Simon and it made my heart sink.

His eyes were like crystals, a beautiful pale almost glowing under the sun's rays. His hair was as blonde as the sand we sat on and came down to his shoulders. His features were simply stunning. He was probably the most attractive man I had ever met.

This man was a god.

"Daphne," he said breathlessly, as he stared at me. His hands moved under my arms and, like it was the most natural thing in the world, he lifted me into the air and spun me around. "I've missed you!"

I couldn't move. I could barely breathe. My mind was blank. It was like nothing I ever felt before. I was lost in his eyes,

Chapter 3

his warmth, and the feeling that I was safe. At that moment, I wished to stay forever. Though I knew better than to remain here. Panic rose in me and I wanted to get away from him, however, my muscles went numb under the warmth of his hands touching me.

He placed me back on the ground and when I gained back my strength I took a step away from him.

"My dear, I have waited for this moment for weeks." His voice was like the wind on a summer day, though there was something off about his tone. Almost like I was dreaming, but I knew I wasn't. Something powerful and dangerous was in his voice.

"Who are you?" I asked.

He looked at me, his lips in a line and eyes drooping. I could only assume he was sad. "Do you not recognize me?" he asked.

I took another step back and shook my head.

He reached forward and grasped my hands. He held them gently, like he was concerned he would scare me. "I am your lost love," he said.

A shocked laugh came from me. "You're not Simon," I said.

"Not entirely," he responded.

I just stared at him, trying to understand what he was saying. I was inexplicably drawn to him. But he wasn't Simon. "I don't understand."

He reached out to push a strand of hair that had fallen in front of my face away. "It's me," he told me. "Just a little different." He smiled and it was like I was seeing Simon again. "Can I kiss you?" he asked.

I stood there for a second before my body betrayed me and nodded. Simon had come back to me.

His face lowered to mine, and he kissed me gently like he was unsure of himself.

I couldn't keep the smile off my face as the kiss sent me on fire with lust. Damn, I wanted him.

He laughed and kissed me again. Still laughing, he murmured, "I love you." I could barely hear the words over the sound of the forest. Those pale eyes devoured me as if I was freedom from a prison only he knew of.

I desperately wanted to be in his arms. But how could I trust this? I pushed him away. There was something both freeing and longing when I no longer felt his touch.

I looked him over. He had on a leather jacket, blue t-shirt, ripped jeans, gray combat boots, and a green bandana on the top of his head. He stood tall over me, 6'3", maybe 6'4". He was built for the forest. Lean enough to maneuver through trees, buff enough to stand toe to toe with any beast. He was so much like Simon yet just different enough that I knew he wasn't him.

His mouth twisted into a smirk, eyes still full of laughter. "It's been a while," he flirted. "Miss me?" As he spoke, he moved closer to me.

"Yes," I said. Then his features looked different again, less like Simon. "Who are you if you are somewhat Simon? Why do you look so different, Simon?" I asked. I didn't understand what he had said. Had something happened to Simon on the quest that made him change so drastically? I needed to know what happened more than I needed to breathe.

"It is me Apollo… I was Simon for many years—but— I died and I reincarnated in my true form once again."

It was like a punch to the stomach. "Died?" I asked, tears welling in my eyes.

He nodded.

My knees buckled and I fell to the ground in a pile of grief.

Chapter 3

Simon was gone. Forever gone. He had died on that damn trip that I told him not to go on. How could he have left me like this? Left me living without him?

I had no reason to stay anymore. I would join Anna's Coalition. I had nothing left keeping me away from it.

The man kneeled before me. He rubbed my shoulder with one hand. "I'm still here, in a way."

I looked him in the eyes. He was so close to being my Simon, but he wasn't. "No!" I said pushing him away.

"I am Simon," he told me. "Just different."

A line from what he said before hit me. *Apollo.* "Simon was Apollo?" I asked.

He nodded.

I shook my head. "But Apollo is Haidar's father."

He nodded. "And that Apollo died after she was born and became Simon."

"Oh." I stared into the woods. "How are you grown?" I asked. "If you reincarnated."

He looked down. "Gods reincarnate as adults sometimes. If we die in the Olympian realm."

"That's where Simon went," I said. His quest was leading him away from Earth and into the Olympian realm to fight back at the growing darkness there.

He took my face in his hands. "It's me," he said. "And you are my Daphne, lost to me for millennia. We are meant to be. That is why we were drawn together."

I removed his hands from me. "You are not my Simon." Then I ran.

I could hear Apollo running after me. "Just listen to me!" he called out.

He would catch me any second, and what then? He thought I

was the woman he lost. He thought he was Simon. I had to do something to stop him from chasing me. Something before he caught me.

"You are my love, I know it." He chased me.

I wanted to turn around and see his expression. I wanted to turn around and see Simon behind me, but I knew it was a bad idea. I could hear his breathing, and soon I would be able to feel it on my neck.

"If I stop, will you leave me alone?" I asked. I needed to cry, to grieve.

Silence. I could feel his nearness. His hand brushed my arm, and I ran faster.

Chapter 4

As I ran I could hear an odd rustling in the trees to my side. Something was there. The rustling sounds grew louder and louder the farther I got into the woods. It made me completely forget about Apollo.

I reached a clearing and stopped. I turned toward the sound of the rustling and a large beast emerged from the woods. My bow appeared in my hand as I stared at the hybrid lion and eagle before me— a griffin.

Apollo came to my side and a bow appeared in his hand as well. We stared at the beast together.

It lunged at us and we both jumped in opposite directions. I rolled across the ground, a cracking sound coming from my ankle. I wouldn't let it stop me. I stood, trying to ignore the pain shooting through my leg.

I aimed my bow and shot at the griffin. The arrow landed in its leg and I smiled at the irony.

Apollo was on the other side of it, shooting at its wings.

Lost Goddess

It turned to him and attempted to catch him in his beak. But Apollo was too quick and moved to the side with perfect precision.

As I watched him, I couldn't help but notice how his movements mimicked Simon perfectly. Maybe he truly was Simon, reborn, coming back to me.

I shot my arrows at the griffin. The first two arrows hit the neck of the griffin and caused it to stumble forward. Then the third arrow went through its eye going into its brain. It fell to the ground, dead.

Apollo rushed over to me and looked me over. "Are you hurt?" he asked.

I pointed at my ankle.

He rested his hands on it.

I pulled away from him. "What are you doing?"

"I'm the god of medicine," he said.

His hands reached for my ankle. I prepared to wince at his touch, but instead, I felt the pain leave me.

I looked at him. How could I have not noticed the small details? A fine line here, a gray hair there, but overall he was still perfect. Perfectly different from Simon and perfectly the same at the same time. "Will you ever let me go?" I couldn't help but ask. I wanted Simon, not an imitation of him.

He moved closer. "You will love me again."

"I will never love you." I had made up my mind. I was joining Anna's Coalition.

He seemed amused by the gesture and leaned in further. We were nose to nose. "Don't kid yourself, you always have." The words bounced off my skin.

I could feel my heart racing. Whether it was fear or something else, I did not know.

Chapter 4

He must have noticed because he softened and moved away barely an inch. "I'm not going to hurt you. I would never harm you. Letting you go was the hardest thing I have ever had to do. Leaving you a second time was just as hard."

"This is wrong." Why did he keep acting like we were lovers? We weren't. Even Simon and I weren't lovers, not yet at least. *Simon is gone, you idiot. He's dead and you can never be with him.*

"Nothing has ever been more right." He caressed my cheek.

"I disagree." My hands found his chest and I shoved him away from me. He landed near my feet.

Before he could speak, a figure came out of the woods. Her hair and smile mimicked that of the man in front of me.

Chapter 5

"Dad?" Haidar asked. Her mother had shown her pictures of her father in Olympian form since she was a kid. Haidar may not have ever met her father, but she could recognize him.

Oh, no. Somehow during this whole time I hadn't thought about how Apollo was her father.

"Haidar," he said with a smile, turning from me to her.

They embraced each other, before Haider looked back at me.

"What happened?" Haidar sat beside me, looking at my ankle.

I wanted to tell her the truth, but I couldn't muster the courage. Telling her, 'Well, your dad was Simon and we were in love. He died and now is in his Olympian form. He pursued me and we fought a griffin together. Now he is healing my ankle and claims to still be in love with me. Also, he thinks I am Daphne,' just didn't sound right.

"Just a broken ankle," Apollo chimed in before I could.

"Good," Haidar said.

Chapter 5

"You keep hunting, my child. My blessing will be with you," he said. "I'll take Dana back to the university."

It was the first time he had called me by my first name and I didn't know if I liked it.

His child walked away slowly and Apollo picked me up. Why? I honestly didn't know. Haidar was nearly out of eyesight when Apollo kissed my cheek. Nearly... but not away just yet. She had seen it, and she would have questions.

The dorms were far from this part of the forest and to get to mine, we would have to walk past most of the other dorms.

Despite the fear of my brothers, quite a few guys at the university had made their interest in me known. While they weren't terrible guys, I never felt the need to date or even the want to. Especially after Anna offered me a place with the women's coalition.

No one would have ever thought to see me with a guy. Especially Phoebus Apollo, but here I was, a helpless maiden.

When Apollo reached the sports fields, I wrapped my arms around his neck tightly and buried my head in his chest. Broken ankle or not, I didn't want anyone seeing me with Apollo, especially in Nike shorts and a tank top. Too many rumors would emerge. Not that hiding my face would help at all. No one at camp had hair like mine.

Apollo, on the other hand, took the motion as an act of endearment and not fear. He kissed the top of my head. *Everyone just saw that,* I thought.

I could hear the whispers as we passed. I could feel Apollo stand up straighter as they grew louder. Almost as though he were proud.

When the ground beneath Apollo seemed to get rough, I opened my eyes. We were almost to my dorm. No one would see us once we were inside. An idea that brought comfort and fear.

He stopped at the door and gently put me down. "I can't enter unless you let me."

"Why?" If he was Simon, he would walk right in. Simon and I had had many movie nights in this room. He wouldn't be wary of entering. Just another reason he wasn't Simon.

"It's decency."

"Alright." I opened the door and invited him in.

He picked me up before I could walk through, however. I entered in his arms, eerily aware of how similar it was to a groom carrying his bride through the threshold.

"Which one's yours?" he asked, looking at the four beds in the room.

I looked around the room myself. Three beds sat on one wall. All of them were small twin sizes. On the other side, sat a full-size bed, my bed.

I pointed to it and Apollo gently sat me down. I snapped my fingers and the lights turned on.

I sat up in the bed, watching Apollo closely as he examined my ankle once more.

He took a small pouch of honey drops and offered it to me. "Eat some. It'll help,"

He sat on the side of the bed, facing me. He then held up some ambrosia and gave it to me to eat.

"You still think that I am the love of your life."

"I know you are, and even if you weren't, then, well, I would still want you." This time he wasn't flirting or smiling. He was pleading with me. "I've seen you. You're gorgeous and smart. You know more about poetry, medicine, and archery than my own children. You're special. I loved you in my past life, I will

Chapter 5

love you in this one."

His children. I had almost forgotten that Haidar was his child. Who knows how many children, from who knows how many lovers, he had. I wasn't going to become another woman he was toying with. And, most definitely, I was not going to betray Haidar by being involved with her dad.

The glow of his eyes seemed to dim. He put his mouth near the point of my ear. "I am a god. We don't give up until we get what we want. I've waited two years. What's a few more weeks?" He moved away from me and stood up. "Good night, Dana. I love you."

Before I could say anything back, he wiped sleep over my eyes.

Chapter 6

Haidar wasn't talking to me after seeing what happened the other day. I didn't blame her, but I wished I could explain that Simon was Apollo, then maybe she would get it, but she wasn't giving me the opportunity.

There was no sign of Apollo for days (and I wasn't complaining about it). Lyle had come up after the incident with the griffin to ensure I was all right, and I worked on my sword skills and hand-to-hand combat.

Lyle wasn't always the easiest to get along with. Mostly because he didn't have a good sense of humor. Sure, he liked stupid humor like stuffing pencils up someone's nose, but not sarcasm.

Nevertheless, I loved him, and he was always there for me. He was one of the only people I could rely on. Besides Haidar and Simon—who was gone now.

***

Chapter 6

It was Sunday morning, and I slept peacefully. Even Lyle's snoring wasn't making me stir.

All was right with the world. No weird gods watching me. No monsters trying to kill me. My life was returning to somewhat normal. The only problem was the hole in my heart that ached for Simon, and the sorrow I felt knowing he was gone.

But because I am the luckiest person in the world (not-so-subtle sarcasm), that all changed.

A knock on the door woke both me and Lyle. He was on his feet before I was, and sword in hand, he walked to the door.

The sun had barely risen, but its pink light was making its way through the windows. *How early was it? 5, maybe 6?* I wasn't sure, but I did know that no one should be up this early.

I wish I were surprised by who was standing at the door. But I wasn't. Right in the doorway was Apollo. He had swapped his leather jacket for a plaid shirt, and his jeans were worn. The same green bandana sat on the head, clashing with the rest of the outfit.

Right now, he looked just like Simon. But I knew that was a lie. He wasn't my dear Simon.

"Ready for our date, I see." He smiled as he looked me over.

I suddenly remembered sleeping in a tight crop top and volleyball shorts. No wonder I felt naked standing there and could feel the blood rush to my cheeks.

When Lyle looked over and saw me, he mouthed the words, "I got this," and walked outside, closing the door behind him.

I ran over to my chest and pulled out some real clothes. Cargo pants with an orange camp t-shirt and Birkenstocks (very stylish, I know).

Then I bravely marched to the door. What I saw... let's just say I would have been less surprised to see a griffin playing basketball. I found my brother and Apollo locked in an arm wrestle.

Dazed with confusion, I asked, "What's going on?"

"Don't worry, when I win this, we can get going on our date," Apollo said. He seemed not to be breaking a sweat.

Lyle, on the other hand, seemed to be practically dying.

"Why are you doing this?" I directed the words at Lyle.

I knew at that moment that I shouldn't have spoken to him. My words made him lose his concentration, and his arm fell beneath Apollo's.

"Well, my love, your brother challenged me to an arm wrestling contest." Apollo's eyes were excited. He walked over to me, put his arm around my waist, and pulled me to his side. "If I won, I could take you out. If he won, I could never see you again."

"You agreed to that." I eyed Lyle.

"It seemed less stupid before," he replied sadly.

"I assume your curfew is still the same?" Apollo asked. I looked into his eyes and realized he was still somewhat Simon. He knew so much about me. There was no lying.

"Yeah..." I didn't want to admit it.

"I'll have her back by 12." He smiled over at Lyle.

Lyle let out a grunt and moved to go inside. Before he got inside, however, he looked over at Apollo, "You better," he muttered and was gone.

Simon had always been honest about his feelings for me, but not like this. Apollo wasn't honest. Honesty meant talking. He was acting on them, and I wasn't sure if I liked it.

Chapter 7

"So, we're leaving the university?" I asked. I didn't leave often.

"Yeah." He smiled at me, and I wasn't sure if I wanted to run or kiss him—

Run you, idiot, I thought, *don't you dare think about kissing him!*

"Where to now?" His voice was smooth, and I could tell he was trying to impress me.

I thought long and hard about where I wanted to go, searching my mind through all my favorite parks and cafes nearby, then it hit me. I told him where and he asked me, "You sure?"

"Positive." I smiled.

When the car stopped, we were in front of a library I knew well. It had been my only escape from the craziness of school and foster homes for years.

Still, the library wasn't why I asked to come here. Behind the library were acres of forest. Public domain to hike on. If I were to leave the university, it would only make sense to come here.

Apollo, on the other hand, did not seem too amused. "Trust me." I smiled.

"Of course." The look in his eyes told me that he felt every moment not touching me was a moment closer he came to death.

Now, I am not one to lead a guy on, but I found myself reaching for his hand. I could tell that he wanted to be closer to me, that holding hands would not be enough, but it was a stretch for me. He would have to deal. Every time we touched before this moment had somehow been his doing. Now I called the shots, and innocently holding hands was all that I could handle.

We walked through the forest rather silently. I listened to every creature around me, including the plants. I always believed that everything in the forest had its song.

I was aware that Apollo gradually came closer to me, but I never realized how close he was until his arm was around my shoulder rather than my hand. "Live in the moment, my love," he told me.

But I didn't want any moments with him. I was still trying to figure out exactly why I came here with him. Why hadn't I stayed at my dorm? Why did I let an unfair arm wrestle determine my day? My question was answered when I saw his eyes. Beaming with warmth and going straight to my soul. I knew what looking at his eyes did to me, so I turned away. "You know, no matter how long I know you, you never seem to want to look me in the eyes," he laughed.

"Maybe if they weren't weapons I would look at them," I scoffed.

"Weapons?" He laughed even louder. "And tell me how they are weapons?"

Chapter 7

"They trick me into desiring you, they hypnotize and force me to do your will. They make me believe you are Simon."

"You have known me for years. Have my eyes ever lured anyone else?" he asked.

I didn't have an answer for him.

"You don't want to look at my eyes because they make you realize what you already feel inside. They make you see that you love me."

"No." I shut my eyes.

"Yes, my dear."

I opened my eyes to find him staring at me. I meet his gaze. Whether he was right or not, I did not know.

Simon had been courteous and gentlemanly. He was terrified of Lyle and never made a move when Lyle was around. Apollo was forward, losing most of his gentleness. I knew they were one and the same, but then how could they be so different?

I looked at him and said, "I liked you more as Simon. How... how did you... become Simon?"

He stopped and turned to me. "Ask what you really mean."

"What are you?" I asked. It was the only question on my mind. What was this man in front of me, if he was a man at all?

He smiled. "Technically the reincarnation of Simon Phoebus.
"

"I know that." I rolled my eyes. "Do you have memories, or powers, from past lives?"

"All of it. I remember it all. I can do it all. Because I reincarnated as my Olympian self, I can change form at will. I couldn't do that as Simon," he said.

"What do you do with it?" I asked.

He stepped towards me. "I spent it looking for you. My dear Daphne. The moment I reincarnated, I began to look for you. But I couldn't come back to you until the veil between the Olympian realm and Earth fell, on the anniversary of the day I lost you."

"But you can go to Olympus on any day," I said.

"But I cannot leave on any day," he told me.

I thought of what he was trying to say. "I'm not Daphne."

"Oh, my dear." His hand caressed my cheek. "You are. It's so hard to control myself around you." His head fell into his hand. "Gods don't have a lot of self-control in our Olympian forms. I don't want to scare you."

"You haven't scared me today, yet," I said, though he had, "Wednesday, on the other hand…" I looked at the ground. "It was so sudden then."

"You're right. I shouldn't have been so forward" He sighed as though he believed himself to be a monster. The conversation paused, then he looked up. "How long?" he asked me.

"What?"

"How long will you make me wait?"

"Wait for what?"

"You… How long until I marry you?"

Eternity, I thought in my head, but that was only what I desired. Apollo had other plans, and I knew the stories. Only death or transformation could save me now. I was on a road to ruin, Apollo my guide. He wasn't going to give up on me. Even if I screamed and shouted that I hated him, he would pursue me. "You're the one who knows the future… I think that was one of Apollo's powers."

"I know fate, and fate is that you will be mine. When however…"

"I don't know." I smiled at him wearily.

He looked down. "You were worried when Simon went

Chapter 7

missing?"

"Yes," I choked. My brain didn't register that Simon was in front of me. Even more, I completely forgot at that moment that Simon and Apollo were the same. In my head, he was a dead friend I hadn't grieved yet.

"You loved him." Apollo wasn't asking. He knew I did. I loved Simon. If he hadn't gone missing, I would have probably never considered Anna's offer.

"I did love him." Tears fell from my eyes. "He just left me, why would he do that?" I looked up at Apollo.

He pulled me to him and let me cry. My head was placed on his chest. He stroked my hair. "You do love me." His voice was sincere and sweet.

I looked up at him, "I loved Simon…"

"I am Simon."

"No! You can't be Simon!" I didn't know where the words came from, but I believed every word. I didn't look at him, my eyes were glued shut, and I didn't want comfort.

"Look at me." His voice was different but recognizable. My eyes opened and Simon was holding me. His eyes did not glow as much as they did in Apollo's form and Simon's hair was slightly darker. One of the most distinct differences was his nose. Simon's was sharp enough to cut rock, and Apollo's was much softer. "I never left you," he told me.

"So you are him." I touched his face.

"It always has been." A tear fell onto my hand from his eyes.

Here he was before me but I still felt myself holding back. Almost as though some supernatural force were stopping me from falling in love. "I can never fully love you."

"The shard." His warm eyes met mine and he put a hand over my heart. "Lead blocks you from loving any man. Eros shot it into you long ago."

I still wasn't sure if I was Daphne, but he was right. I couldn't truly love anyone completely romantically, not just him. I loved Simon, but not enough to be with him.

"Come to Olympus. I may be able to heal you there." His forehead touched my own.

I suddenly realized that I was fully cradled in his arms but I didn't care. Every moment with my lost friend, god or not a god, meant something.

"I can't." I looked at him.

"I can return to Olympus and live there, and I can bring you with me, make you a goddess again." Suddenly, he was Apollo again and his voice was stern and powerful. "Anna says you still want to join her coalition?" He looked at me. "As long as I claim you, she cannot let you pledge to her."

"So I need permission?" I leaped from his arms, tears gone. This was the type of god I knew. Rash, harsh, selfish. All that stuff about loving me was a ploy. And I could never love him back.

"In mortal terms, yes!"

"So I have no choice. I choose you or, well, my only option is you!"

"Indeed it is."

"Then you are no better than a slave master and me no more than a slave."

"I do this because I love you!"

"If you loved me, you would set me free."

"If you didn't have that lead in your heart, you wouldn't want me to set you free."

"I'm not Daphne! I wasn't born thousands of years ago. I wasn't revived. I am not your long lost love! I am the daughter

Chapter 7

of Iris, god of color and communication, nothing more."

"Yes, you are, I know it."

I forcefully pushed him away from me. "You know nothing!" The moment I said it, I knew it was going to bite me in the butt.

I saw no gentleness in his eyes. No warmth, either. As he approached me, his form changed back to Apollo. He grabbed my arm. "You, a mortal, dare disrespect a god!"

As he released me, I fell backward onto my not-fully-healed ankle. "You!" The pain made tears form in my eyes. "You said you wouldn't harm me."

I don't think dropping the Empire State Building on him could have hurt him more. It was like he had come out of a daze. Within seconds, he was by my side, trying to console me and heal my ankle.

"Get away!" I screamed.

"I'm so sorry!" He seemed more distraught than me.

"Just take me home." I was done with him. I never wanted to look at him again.

"I understand."

With a snap of his fingers, we were back in the dorm sitting on my bed. "You can teleport?"

"I'm an Olympian, not mortal."

"Oh, yeah." I rolled my eyes.

"How about a movie?" Suddenly a large TV appeared on top of Lyle's bed.

"I want to be alone."

"Nope." He looked at me and smiled sincerely. "I'm going to make up for what I did."

"I said get out!" All I wanted was to be alone. To sleep, to forget that he existed. Forget Apollo existed, even forget that Simon existed.

His arm wrapped around me. "Your eyes glow when you're mad."

"I know." I met his gaze. It was a side effect of being the child of an Olymian god. He knew that, why he drew attention to it, I did not know.

The look in his eyes showed true regret. "I'm sorry, I couldn't bear the thought of losing you. I went mad."

"So will you give your blessing for me to join the coalition?" I asked.

He pulled me close to him and I knew the answer. "No, but it's to protect you more than for my gain," he promised.

"You mind going?" I still wanted to be alone.

"Why do you insist I leave?"

"Honestly, I just want to sleep." There was no hiding or denying it. I was nearly falling over.

"I'll sleep on the ground," he said.

"I asked you to leave." I was done with all his antics and just the sight of him was making me angry.

He hesitated, then met my eyes. "All right. I'll see you soon."

Chapter 8

It was a month later and Apollo's visits were frequent. Three days a week, at least. He still, of course, tried to persuade me to come to Olympus with him. I never accepted. Obviously.

I didn't know how, but he seemed to be becoming more gentle as time passed. He had begun to give me more personal space when we walked together, just talking like friends would. I felt like the further space he let me put between us, the closer I wanted to be to him. *Stop it!* I told myself. Falling for Apollo was not part of my plan.

We would talk about our families and lives. I mentioned my life growing up in foster care with Haidar and meeting Lyle at Lakefield Prep Academy where he was my teacher and then later discovering he was my brother. I told him more details about Anna's offer, to which he cringed. "You know that as long as I claim you, she cannot accept you." She was his twin. Helping me get free from him would be betraying him.

Lost Goddess

On top of these visits, Apollo kept visiting my dreams. Each night he would visit me while I slept and try to persuade me not to join Anna, to let him take me to Olympus, or just to talk, even. I could have sworn I awoke to find him sitting on my bed watching me, or feel his arms holding me, numerous times.

Every time this happened, it was the same. I would dream about him. He would plead with me. Then, I finally opened my eyes. It didn't matter if he was holding me or watching me, he always said, "Good night, I love you," and disappeared.

* * *

When I awoke this morning something was different. When I dreamed, he seemed scared. He warned me about someone… "A," I think he said. I can't completely remember who, then when I woke up, there was nothing.

Even on nights I didn't see him, I would find an arrow next to me, or some other sign. But nothing at all. I couldn't help but feel that he might be in danger.

I know if he was, I shouldn't care. He was a god who relentlessly pursued me. His being gone should be great… but yet part of me felt like I should help him. Find him.

Finding Anna was quite easy.

I knew the coalition headquarters were somewhere in the Austin hills.

"Finally made up your mind?" A woman walked up to me.

I wanted to say yes and pledge myself to Anna's coalition right then and there, but I knew I couldn't. Apollo needed my help and for whatever reason, I was going to save him.

"I need to speak with Anna," I began.

"Then speak, child." A young woman came out from behind

Chapter 8

some doors at the small airport. I barely recognized Anna.

I told her the story... all of it. She cringed every time I mentioned her brother kissing or even touching me.

"I have known my brother was reincarnated as his true self and went away, but I didn't know..." she began. "Who would take him?"

"Are we sure someone even took him?" I asked.

She nodded. "He would not stay away from you this long, not even in mortal form, much less in his Olympian state. The darkness must have seeped into earth."

"The darkness he died—*Simon died* trying to fight?" I asked. She nodded.

Now we were sitting inside her cabin. The fire in the hearth reminded me of Apollo's eyes. I couldn't help but miss him.

"Does anyone have a grudge against him?" I asked. "Anyone that could easily be subdued and controlled by the darkness?"

She laughed. "He is beloved by all Olympians, the charmer." I could hear the annoyance in her tone.

"Then what happened?"

The fire roared and it sounded like a laugh.

We both turned to it as the flames turned black.

Another laugh rose from the flames. "My dear," the flame said. "All you had to do was ask."

I didn't recognize the voice, but Anna did.

"Aphrodite!" Anna roared.

"Yes," the flames said. "And I think I have something you want."

"Where is Apollo?" the words flowed out of my mouth without thought.

"Come see me and find out," she said. Then the flames turned back to their orange hue.

Anna looked at me. "Aphrodite is a reporter in NYC. Always looking for a good story even if she has to make it herself. I think that's how the darkness overcame her. Now it wants to overcome Apollo." She looked at the fire. "You have to save him. Your love could overcome the darkness."

"I'll do it." The words slipped from me. *Anything for Apollo.* I didn't know why I felt this way but I did. I would die for him if I had to.

I was beginning to love him back. Although the thought terrified me, it was true. I felt something more than obligation. I wanted to find him. I wanted to be near him. I had to save him.

Before I left to find Aphrodite's palace, Anna put a hand on my shoulder, "My dear, I want nothing more than you to join my coalition. We do great work here." She seemed to be regretting every word she spoke. "But I hope you know that unless he releases you, letting you be a member would mean I would be betraying him."

"I know." Another reason I had to find Apollo. Whether I loved him or not, I still wished to be a member and I would have to beg for his blessing.

Chapter 9

I thought Aphrodite's penthouse would be harder to find, but it wasn't. Anna had told me it lay outside of NYC and was glowing with her power, but I didn't fully understand until I saw it.

The building seemed to be carved out of pure marble. Thirty-foot arches surrounded the building along with a collection of gorgeous statues.

I hadn't even knocked or rung the doorbell when Aphrodite opened the door, smiling wide. "You've made it."

"Um, yeah." I nodded, terrified of what came next.

She wore a silk dress that fell to the floor. Her makeup and hair were perfect. Outwardly, she was the most gorgeous being in the world, yet there was an ugliness to her, like an old woman who overdid the Botox.

"Ready for your first trial?" her eyes shined as she spoke.

"Trial?" I asked.

She gave a sadistic laugh. "You want to fight me, you have to prove your love."

'No', I wanted to say but couldn't. All I did was shake my head.

She led me through her home into a dark room. When the lights flickered on, I saw a ten-foot pile of seeds sitting before me.

"Have them sorted by sundown," she said, closing the door behind herself.

I couldn't help myself. The task was impossible, panic rose within me.

As I cried, an ant crawled over my arm. I remembered something about Psyche's story. *The ants saved her.* I took a good look at my friend on my arm. "Do you think your colony could help me? I would give you food for your troubles. I am trying to save the man I—love." I reached into my pocket and held out a cookie I had taken before I left the coalition.

I could have sworn the ant nodded her head at me before climbing off of me.

I waited over an hour before the ants arrived, but they worked quickly enough to make up for it. Before I could blink my eye, the pile was perfectly sorted by type of seed.

Aphrodite returned soon after. Her face twisted darkly as she looked over me. It was like a wall was between us, something separating me from her darkness.

She gave me no rest before my second trial. To fetch golden wool from the golden rams in one of the magic forests near the entrance to the Olympian realm. They were known to be feisty creatures and I was terrified at the prospect of approaching one.

Just traveling there took a whole day, a whole day's time that I shouldn't have wasted.

Luckily I had learned how to think with little rest, and

Chapter 9

remembered how Psyche gathered the wool. She waited for the rams to go through the bushes and took the wool off the thorns of the bushes.

When the task was complete and I arrived at Aphrodite's penthouse again she welcomed me with open arms. I was honored with a feast and a place to rest.

"So where is he, exactly?" I asked Aphrodite.

"My dear, eat! You will know soon enough." She smiled and I could have sworn her eyes turned black.

"Where is he!" My voice was firm. I didn't just spend three days undergoing trials to come out empty-handed.

Something in my voice must have startled the darkness inside her because it seemed like she was awoken from a daze. "An island in the south Pacific," she said slightly.

I could feel the magic swirling around me as I spoke to her. I could feel the darkness around her quiver as I stood and walked closer to her. It was no match for love. "No!" I muttered to myself. I stalked up to her and grabbed a knife from the table and brought it to her throat. "Bring him here now."

"I can't...," she began. "It won't let me," she whispered.

I pushed the knife harder. "Now. I am the only thing here that you need to fear."

Before I could blink an eye, Apollo was sitting in front of me. He looked dizzy, and I thought it must've been from the transformation, but then he fell into my arms and passed out.

I growled, "What did you do to him?"

"I did nothing," she said through a giggle, her eyes growing black again. "The darkness poisoned him."

Chapter 10

NEVER, even in a life-and-death situation, do I recommend carrying a man twice your size.

Even poisoned, he was finding ways to be in my arms. I laughed at the thought. When I looked at his face, I saw how peaceful he was when sleeping in the ambulance to the hospital. Even unconscious, Apollo radiated a warmth that made me want to be near him forever. *Snap out of it.*

"He's been poisoned," I muttered sleepily to the EMT outside of Aphrodite's building. I realized at that moment that I hadn't slept in nearly four days. Even so, there was no time to rest now. Apollo still needed my help.

As I watched Apollo sleep on the hospital bed, it was like seeing him for the first time. Every feeling of anger and contempt I ever had for him was gone. Nothing was left in their place but admiration—and love.

I stayed there as long as I could. It was probably one-thirty in the morning when Lyle came and dragged me to bed. Before

Chapter 10

I went with him, I leaned over and kissed Apollo on the head, "Goodnight, I love you." I meant the words with all my heart. He was mine. Simon or Apollo, he was still the love of my life.

* * *

The second I felt the sun coming through the windows, I leaped out of bed and ran to the street to find a taxi to take me back to the hospital.

I had to tell Apollo I loved him and nothing else mattered. It only took a few seconds for reality to catch up with me. When I reached the street, I realized that everyone was watching me.

I shrugged off the feeling of embarrassment and kept waiting, however. The second I arrived at the hospital room, I slammed open the door and walked in.

It took me a second to realize that the entire room was empty besides me... and a shirtless Apollo who I had walked in on in the middle of changing.

"Hi," he smiled, letting the shirt in his hands drop to the floor. "Your outfit. Oversized shirt and leggings are interesting choices." He laughed.

He was exactly right. That was all I was wearing... A thin oversized shirt (one of Lyle's that he had brought). It was so long on me that I could have worn it back at Lakefield Constructive Academy (my very conservative highschool) as a dress and no one would bat an eye. The tight leggings I wore cut off at my knees.

I couldn't talk, I couldn't move. All I did was look at him and pray he didn't notice how hard it was for me not to blush.

"You're cute when you're nervous," he said.

Even though Apollo was still smiling, he wasn't flirting, not even in the slightest.

I approached him, "What about yourself? It can't be comfortable for you without a shirt." It wasn't comfortable for me, either.

He smirked, "What? Do I make you uncomfortable?"

There he was, my man.

"Yeah," I squeaked.

He seemed to cringe at the words rather than enjoy them. He looked down at his feet, seeming ashamed. "Thanks for saving me," he said earnestly, but I could tell he wasn't done talking. "I think being around you made the darkness subside." He sat down on his bed and looked up at me. Whatever he was thinking was killing him inside. "I... I... I realized something." He looked up at me and I could see the pain as he spoke,

"I did, too—" I muttered, but he cut me off.

"It's not loving for me to stop you from joining my sister's coalition just because I want you for myself." Every word sounded like someone had staved him through the heart. "There is some time left before her deadline. You have my blessing to join her." A tear streaked his face. I never knew gods could cry until now.

I could feel my breathing get heavy... *Had he really just said those words? Had he really let me go?* It all seemed like a dream. A month ago, I would have left him and joined the hunt at that second, but now... I loved him. I wanted to be with him. I would give up the coalition in a second if it meant I could be with him.

I looked at him and saw the pain in his eyes. In his mind, he had just lost me for a third time. Something he once told me was the most difficult thing he was ever forced to do, and now he wasn't even forced, he was willing. He was willingly putting

Chapter 10

my desire before his own... *Had I ever heard of a god doing that? I don't think so.*

"Thank you." The words seemed to crush him like I had just affirmed that I was leaving him.

His head was in his hands and I walked over to him.

"Look up," I told him and he did so. "Now stand up, you idiot." I smiled.

When he did, I reached my arms around his neck. "I realized something too," I kissed him gently so that he wouldn't be too off guard.

"I thought—" He looked at me skeptically.

I smiled. "I did say thank you, but I didn't accept the offer."

He smiled at me, "What does that mean exactly?" he asked.

"It means I'm yours." I looked at him with as much longing as he did me. "Forever. I love you." I wanted to marry him—Simon or Apollo, or just as Apollo. I want to be his wife. It was like I had just pushed down a wall in my heart. Suddenly I felt something inside my hand.

"Finally," he murmured before kissing me. We both loved each other, and we both wanted each other. The man in my arms was my love and I couldn't be happier.

The moment ended suddenly when Haidar walked into the room. When I saw who interrupted us, I was terrified she would be angry at me, but she only smiled. "You going to be my new mom?" she asked happily.

That idea kinda grossed me out, but I could tell that she didn't mean for me to take it like that. She was happy for me and more than that she was happy about the situation.

"That depends." Apollo smiled. He got down on one knee, "Will you be my wife, not just a mortal one, but my wife on Olympus?"

"That depends." I smiled, "How special am I compared to your mortal lovers?"

"I have loved you for thousands of years." He kissed my hand and a ring appeared on my finger and I noticed that whatever was in my fist disappeared.

My eyes watered as I stared at the ring on my hand. The center stone in the ring was a piece of lead, it had come out of my heart when I decided I wanted to marry him. That's what I had felt in my hand. That was the wall I had felt crumble inside me. The lead from the arrow Eros had put in my was gone.

"No one else can compare," he said.

"You're already assuming I am gonna say yes," I teased.

He stood up and wrapped his arms around me. "You did say you are mine forever."

"True," I smiled and pecked his cheek, extremely aware that Haidar was next to us.

"I think, I'll leave you two alone," she said, and headed towards the door.

"You don't have to." Apollo smiled at her. "You girls, you have a wedding to plan."

"An Olympian wedding." My stomach churned at the thought.

"I think I could convince my sister to help, if you wanted?" he asked, but he already knew my answer.

"That would be amazing." I kissed him again before he left.

"Roses or tulips?" Haidar asked the second he was out the door.

"Laurels." I smiled at her.

Chapter 11

One thing I didn't know about Olympian weddings was how quick they were to plan. I had barely been engaged for a day before Anna came to my rescue, putting together all the details in a mere three hours.

"For a maiden goddess, you know a lot about weddings," I teased. Since she was nearly my sister, I felt like it wasn't inappropriate to address her so casually.

"Well, maidens make the best bridesmaids and bridesmaids plan the weddings." She smiled at me, "It does help that this wedding is special. For thousands of years, my brother could never settle down, never give me a sister, now he has."

"So you've been planning this day in your head for years?" I asked. I was standing on a pedestal while some minor god I forgot the name of circled around me pinning my dress in place.

"Yes."

I was happy to finally have a sister, although she was a god and not on Olympus much. I could tell she would be there if I ever needed help.

"One last question." my voice grew low. "If you forsake all men, and encourage others to do so, too… then why are you so happy for me?"

She seemed unphased by my question. "Multiple reasons. To start, Apollo isn't some man, he's my brother. He's Apollo and who am I to say the cause of his joy is wrong? Also, forsaking all men does not apply to every woman. If it did, then there would be no children in the world."

"Huh," was all I could manage to say before my seamstress's hand slipped, stabbing me with a needle. "Ahh!" I screamed, before leaving the room to stop the bleeding from damaging the dress.

* * *

It was probably eleven at night when a knock made me jump awake from bed.

I opened the door and to no surprise, Apollo stood there. He stared at me calmly

"What are you doing here? It's bad luck," I teased.

"I had to see you." He smirked at me. His eyes moved from my head to my feet. I knew that in a day he would be my husband, but I still felt uncomfortable with him seeing me in pajamas.

"You'll see me tomorrow." I tried to shut the door on him, but he held it open.

"True, but I wanted to see if you wanted to stay mortal after tomorrow or not?"

"All right."

"I've been thinking… do you want kids?" he asked.

Chapter 11

"Of course," I replied, nervous at what came next.

"I do, too… but… tomorrow you're an Olympian god. It becomes much more difficult after that."

"Weren't both your parents gods?"

"Yes, but… it could be thousands of years for us."

I placed a hand on his arm, in a vain attempt to comfort him. "Then we wait." I kissed his cheek, "I need to go to sleep. I love you."

"I love you, too." It was clear the conversation hadn't made him feel any better.

He turned to leave and, when the door finally closed behind him, I allowed a few tears to streak my face. He didn't just want me. He wanted a family. A life together. Raising children and all.

Slowly I made my way to the bed and fell asleep. I wish I could say it was a peaceful night, but lying has never been something I am particularly good at.

Chapter 12

"Wake up!" a voice yelled at me and I sprung from my bed ready for battle.

The most dangerous thing I found, though, was Haidar holding a camera and huntresses filled my room.

"Why?" I was never a morning person and it now seemed to be the middle of the night. When I glanced at the clock it read midnight. Only an hour after Apollo had visited me.

"You're coming to Olympus so we can finish your preparations." Anna giggled.

"But sleep?"

"You will sleep plenty, just in my home."

"All right."

* * *

I didn't remember how or what happened on Olympus that morning. Something about last-minute dress fitting. Aphrodite

Chapter 12

(who apparently was saved from the darkness by her husband Hephaestus) sent her personal assistant to do my hair.

Hera needed to bless the ceremony. It was all a bit much for my taste.

Around four in the morning, I was allowed to sleep again, but only briefly. I found that gods have no understanding about a mortal's need for rest. The bridesmaids woke me up at six to prepare for the ceremony.

No one really let me in on the decoration planning. So I was nervous coming up to the ceremony knowing nothing of how well plans were going.

At ten I was all ready. Lyle showed up and escorted me to the garden that hosted the ceremony. Large oak doors stood between me and the wedding. This was it. I was going to marry Apollo.

The doors creaked open slowly and my heart beat faster and faster. The venue was gorgeous. Roses and wildflowers covered the garden. The roof was dripping in gorgeous vines of every color. Gods and creatures of all kinds lined the seats, I don't think I could name them all if I tried.

Across from me at the altar stood Apollo shining bright. He wore a bright red suit that surprisingly matched the rest of the wedding. He looked at me and I could tell he was just as nervous. However, the closer I got to him, the better I felt. He was familiar and a source of stability. The more I thought about it, the less scared I became.

I reached the altar and Lyle left me. I stared into Apollo's eyes. "Worth the thousand years of wait?"

"Always." He smiled.

Zeus officiated the ceremony (the only way to make it official in the eyes of the gods). The vows were fairly standard; love, cherish, all that stuff.

What surprised me was what Apollo added. After the rings he looked straight into my eyes. "I swear to remain faithful forever. No one but you for eternity. No more children but yours. Only you, my lovely wife"

I was shocked. I hadn't thought about it that much. Most of the gods were married and still had mortal affairs leading to demigod children. I nodded in amazement and said. "I swear to be faithful to you for eternity." I was 99% sure the crowd looked at us with awe.

"I pronounce you husband and wife, Mr. and Mrs. Phoebus Apollo."

"Apollo." I chuckled at him.

"Dana's not that common," Apollo snapped back jokingly.

"You may kiss!" Zeus was obviously ignoring us.

In front of everyone we just had a small peck, but it meant the world. Finally I was his and he was mine. Nothing would come between us again. Apollo pulled a small pouch from his pocket and offered it to me. "Ambrosia."

I took it from him and put it away. "Keep it. How about a kid?"

Joy filled his face and he kissed me for real this time. I don't think he cared that everyone saw. I don't think I cared that everyone saw.

The reception was great, but honestly the transition of ceremony to reception was a blurry mess. One second I was walking away from the altar. The next, I was dancing in Apollo's arms and eating cake.

When it was time to leave, I was ready. Unlike the gods, I needed rest. As I approached the door, I realized that I had forgotten something. With a swift motion my bouquet flew

Chapter 12

into the air. Haidar caught the bouquet which made her date (Jacque, son of Hephaestus) a little too happy.

"Don't get any ideas." Apollo glared at him, "That's my daughter."

As we were leaving, Haidar hugged me which made my ribs nearly break. "See you soon, Mom." She smiled.

"I will never be able to accept that. "You are my best friend, that's it."

"Bye, Mom," she teased.

It was hard to see her walk away. It was even more difficult when I realized that I would never play capture the flag with her again. Or be able to win a chariot race by her side.

Almost as though he could read my thoughts, Apollo pulled me close. "Couple thousand years and it won't hurt as much."

* * *

I thought that being married to a god would stop people from interrupting my sleep. I was very wrong.

A week after the wedding, I was sleeping soundly in bed when a powerful knock on the door woke both of us. I looked over at the clock and it read 6:10. Too early for a human to function.

"Too early to do anything," I murmured and stuffed my head under the pillows.

Apollo seemed to get the hint because he kissed my cheek and got up to open the door.

"Dad?" he said in a tired voice as he opened the door.

"We need to talk." Zeus' voice was firm and I leaped from the bed.

"About?" Apollo sounded bitter.

"Your ambition to make your wife a god," Zeus said sternly.

Lost Goddess

"Is that a problem?" Apollo's manner was unchanging.

"Well… both of you, come to the throne room."

* * *

In the throne room, I was the only one standing. Apollo being a major god had his own throne and I did my best not to be bitter that he left me. Seeing your new husband as a fifteen-foot giant is quite intimidating.

Standing there alone I felt like I was being put on trial. Every god was looking at me, watching me, whispering about me. I attempted to keep my eyes on my husband, but that failed as he appeared to be speaking intensely to Anna.

"So what is the problem?" Apollo asked as he looked over to Zeus. It was apparent that he was still sleepy and I knew all he wanted was to go back to bed.

"Your new wife, Dana." Zeus said my name as though he had never met me, much less that I was standing in the same room. "When she was born as Daphne, she was a naiad. A minor god, my son."

"I am aware." Apollo's eyes grew narrow.

"She was the minor god of color and forest. Now she is no more than a mortal." I flinched at the sound of his voice. The words "minor" and "mortal" were never compliments.

"Not for long," Apollo told him.

"Oh, yes, you're waiting to make her an Olympian god. All this 'gods rarely have children' business stopping her from becoming a god." Zeus scoffed. "I have it from a reliable source that she is already with child, so you may proceed with your plans. That is, if—"

Apollo kept his stare firmly on his father, as did I, but from

Chapter 12

the corner of my eye, I saw him wink at me. He was just as happy about this information as I was. If I wasn't so nervous I would have probably leaped for joy. Instead, all I did was clench my stomach. "All right, then, we will get to making her a god," Apollo said and Zeus eyed his son suspiciously.

"You probably wish to make her an Olympian, I assume," Zeus responded.

The words scared even Apollo, "No, no, we..." he stuttered through the words.

I could barely breathe. An Olympian was far from anything I ever wanted. I wouldn't even want to be a god if it wasn't so important to Apollo.

Zeus clapped his hands together, causing a shock of electricity to fill the room. With a chuckle, he looked at Apollo. "Demeter has already offered to step down so Dana could join us."

Apollo's eyes grew wide. He turned to Demeter. "Really?" It was not a question of misunderstanding but astonishment.

Demeter looked to me calmly. "Harvest is no longer celebrated as it once was. I am not appreciated or special anymore. Slowly, I fade away. The forest, however, is still loved and cared for by growing conservation. Color, as well, is more popular now. Western culture has changed. Now is your time."

My heart leaped. My feet wanted to run. Being an Olympian was more than I ever asked for. However, I did not respond in time. "We agree," Apollo spoke for me.

My eyes turned to darts as I looked at him. "I'm not..."

Apollo walked to me, shrinking back to normal size as he grew closer, "You will be great."

"Bbbbbut... I never even wanted to be a god." Tears formed in my eyes. I wasn't sure if they were joy or fear. "Me, an Olympian? I can't."

Lost Goddess

Apolo pulled me into his arms, "My love, nothing would make me happier."

"I have to, don't I…" I looked into his eyes.

He stared at the ground, the joy leaving his eyes. "Yes…"

I then realized that this was not an offer but a present being given to me. I pulled the ambrosia from my pocket. "Should I?"

He smiled happily. "You're ready."

I ate the ambrosia. I didn't feel any different. But based on the glowing of my skin, I must have looked it.

A light covered me from head to toe and I rose into the air. As I began my descent back to the ground, I saw a dress of green leaves and vines had covered me and flowers appeared in my hair, which now reached the floor in an intricate braid. "I… am I wearing leaves?"

"Yes." Apollo looked at me like I was more gorgeous than Aphrodite, which she must have noticed based on her jealous stare from across the room.

"How do I change?" I asked him nervously.

"Will it," he told me.

It was an odd experience. All I did was think about what I wished to look like and it happened. Suddenly I was in my favorite cargo pants, combat boots, and black crop top (I called it my *Kim Possible look*). I felt so much more like myself and my hair was back to normal. Demeter stood up from her throne and offered it to me. "You sure?" I asked.

"Positive." She smiled.

As I walked to her, I willed myself to grow larger and I did. By the time I reached her, I was a giant like the rest of them. Demeter's throne was covered in plants (mostly crops). The second I sat down, however, the whole thing changed. Bright green leaves and a thousand colored flowers sprouted.

Chapter 12

"You look perfect," Apollo murmured.

I blushed. I still wasn't sure about this whole Olympian thing, but now it was done.

Life as an Olympian was amazing and awful. On one hand, I had a true home forever. A husband who loved me and a strong son, Paris (minor god of color and art), and, as goddess of the forest, I spent quite a bit of time with the hunters and Haidar.

On the other hand, I spent many days in the Olympian throne room listening to everyone fight about whether hot Cheetos or original were better (there was a full twelve-day council to address it) and another seven-day council on whether toasted Cheez-its were morally just to eat (turns out by Olympian god opinion, they are not), and other council meetings to discuss other similar important issues.

My life is not what I expected at all, yet I still love it.

Printed in the USA
CPSIA information can be obtained
at www.ICGtesting.com
LVHW060552041023
759781LV00092B/2919

9 781088 128930